P9-DYY-809

Emily Tetri

TIGER -VS.- NIGHTMARE

:01
First Second
New York

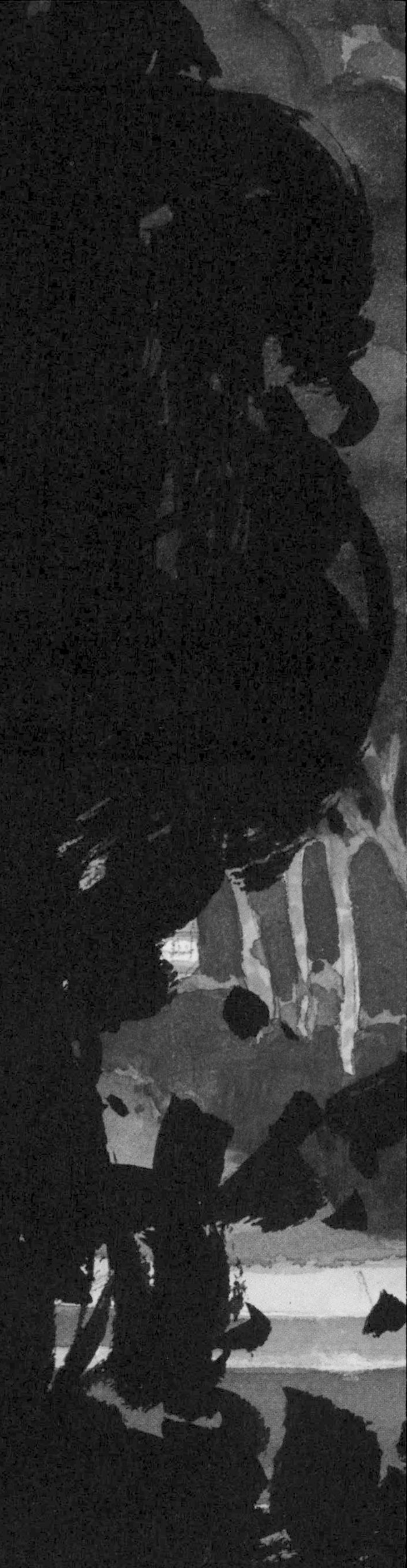

To Mom, Dad, and Laura, who all
helped me fend off many nightmares

:01
First Second

Published by First Second

First Second is an imprint of Roaring Brook Press, a division
of Holtzbrinck Publishing Holdings Limited Partnership

175 Fifth Avenue, New York, NY 10010

Library of Congress Control Number: 201795418

ISBN: 978-1-62672-535-5

Our books may be purchased in bulk for promotional, educational,
or business use. Please contact your local bookseller or the Macmillan
Corporate and Premium Sales Department at (800) 221-7945 ext. 5442
or by e-mail at MacmillanSpecialMarkets@macmillan.com.

First edition, 2018

Book design by Andrew Arnold and Rob Steen

Painted with Prima Marketing and Windsor & Newton watercolors
on Arches watercolor paper. Penciled with Papermate and Tomato
mechanical pencils. Digital editing and assembly in Photoshop.

Printed in China by Toppan Leefung Printing Ltd., Dongguan City, Guangdong Province

10 9 8 7 6 5 4 3 2 1

Dad? Can I be excused?

Yes, Tiger. You **may**.

And **may** I have some extra food for the monster under my bed?

Sure, but make sure your "monster" doesn't leave a mess, or you'll be cleaning up monster messes in the morning.

Thanks!
My monster never leaves messes!

Oh, they're so cute at that age!

Oh yes, Tiger is always coming up with these stories!
I think she's just growing—always hungry.

Y'know...

The grown-ups
think you're
just in my
imagination.

Ooo, curry!
Thanks!

Do you really think we'd get to hang out and play every night if they knew I was real?

Hmm, yeah. Good point.

Are you done with that curry yet?
We still have to finish our game from last night!

FANG WASH
STRIPES & COAT

The next day

I'm home!

We're in the shop!

So, this monster of yours—is it scary?
No! It's my friend!
And how long have you had a monster for a friend?

Welllll...I don't know exactly.

As long as I can remember?

I know it was supposed to come scare me when I was a baby...
...but Monster said it didn't seem fair to scare a baby.
Monsters gotta scare **something**, though.
So it started scaring away my nightmares for me.

So now, I usually bring it some dinner,
and we play games,
and then when I go to sleep, it keeps the nightmares away.
Ah, so we're feeding a monster as well as a daughter, eh?

If it's keeping the nightmares away, it's probably worth it.
Definitely.
NOD
Does your monster have any dinner requests?

It loves curry!
And tacos!

It's not so into stew though.

Huh. Funny how those line up with your favorites.

Daaaad! Those line up with **most** people's favorites.
Stew is terrible.
I like stew.

That night
Do you need us to check under the bed for monsters?
No! I told you, Monster is my friend.

Right, right! Silly us.

Well, remind your monster to brush its teeth after dinner!
Shut!

And so, things continued...

...as they always had.

Every night, Monster would eat...

...they would play...

...and Monster would
fend off nightmares.

Always the same routine.

Monster scared away
the nightmares with ease.

shoo.

Get out of here. I'm not afraid of you!

THWACK!

OW.

I'm sorry...

The next morning, Tiger was confused.

The last time she had a nightmare, Monster had been on vacation.

She'd have to wait until nighttime to ask what happened. Monster was never around during the day.

It was a very sleepy day.

poke

So, did you...

...did you go somewhere last night?

Ummmm.

I had a nightmare last night.

And you keep those away.

Where were you?

I, umm...
I don't know.

I guess one slipped through somehow.
Don't worry; it won't happen again.

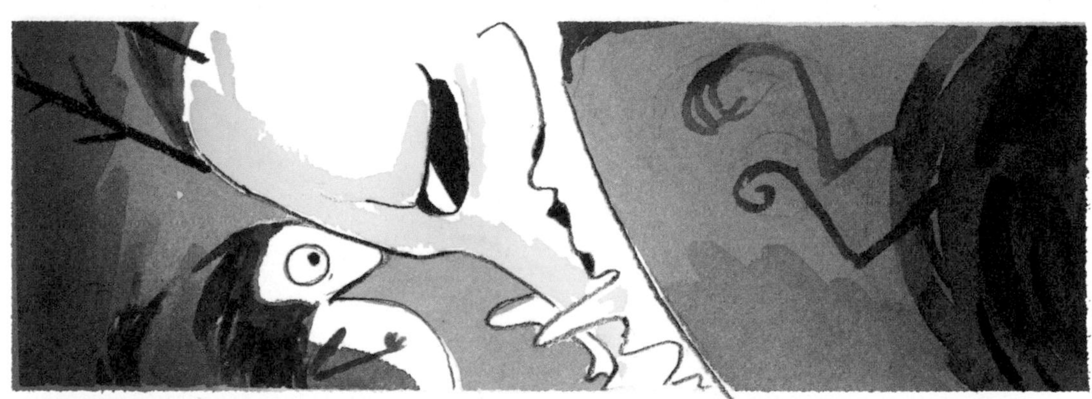

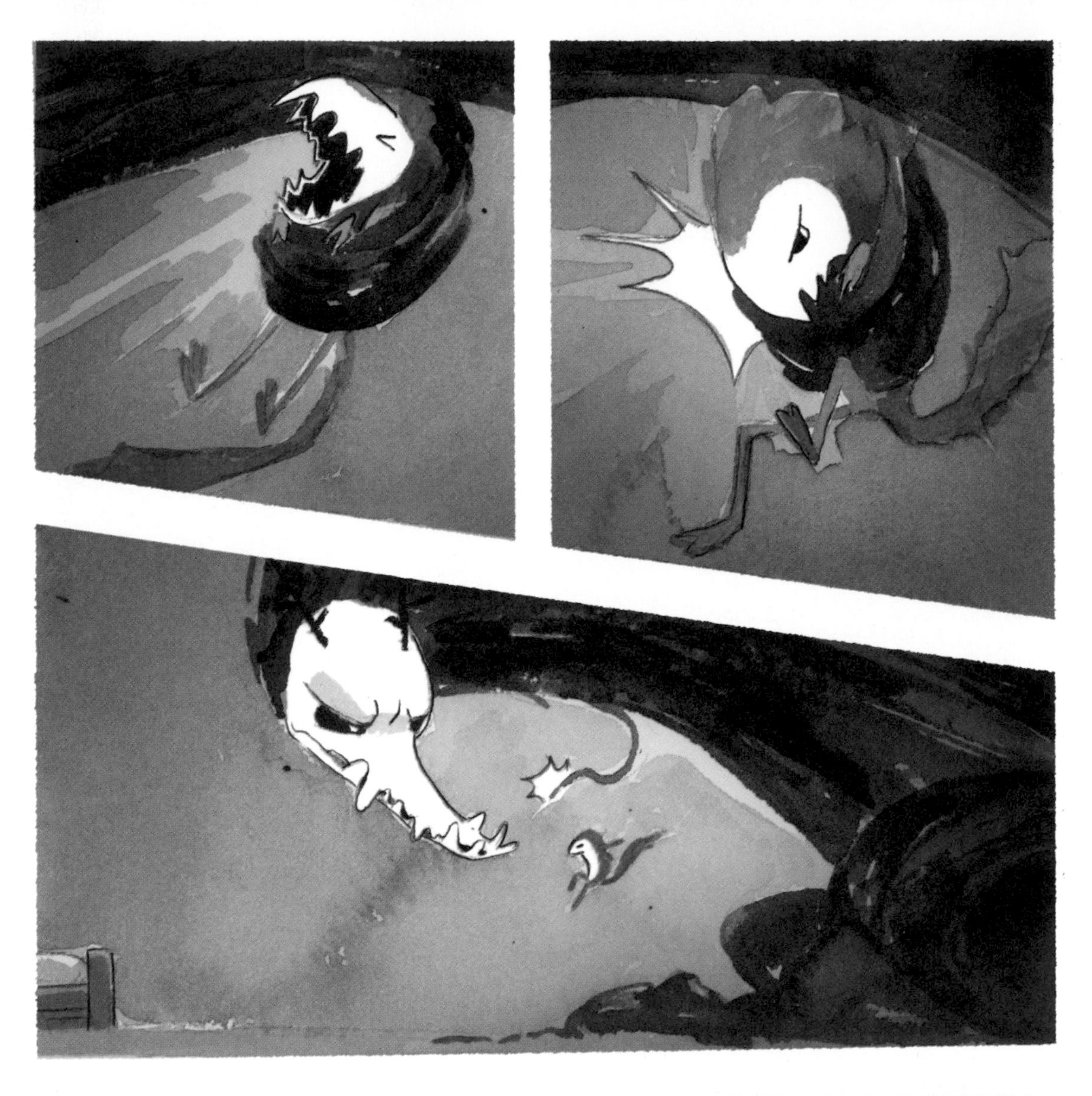

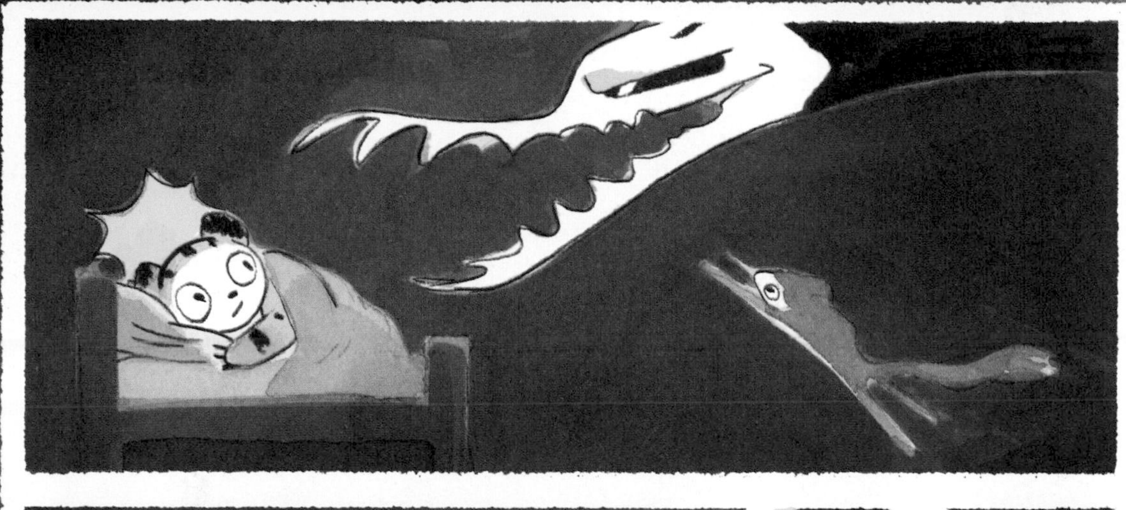

QUICK!
Get under the covers!

Okay. I think we're safe under here.

The next night
Okay.

Soothing tea for easy sleep?
Check!

Relaxing bedtime stories for sweet dreams?
Check!

And I found armor for you!

Helmet!
Shield!
Shin guards!
Sword!

YOU
GOT
THIS!

Nope.

The next night, Tiger
didn't know what to do.

Hmm... Y'know...

Well, it's just that...

...it's coming from your mind, right? All nightmares do.

I know.
I know it can't actually hurt me.

But even so, when it shows up, it's so scary.
Yeah, it is. It's weird how that works.

Okay.
I can do this.
It's my turn.

They came up with a plan.

You're in my head.
YOU'RE
NOT
REAL.

WHOOOSH!

You're in my head!
You're not real!

See?
WHOOOOSH!

Huh...?

HAH!

YOU'RE

NOT

REAL!

pop!

phew
ROAR!

From that night on...
...they would play games...

...fend off nightmares...

...and go to sleep.
Both of them.